First published in Great Britain in 2009
by Piccadilly Press, Ltd.

Library of Congress Cataloging-in-Publication Data
is available from the Library of Congress.
ISBN: 978-0-8075-4636-9

10 9 8 7 6 5 4 3 2 1 WK 15 14 13 12 11 10

For more information about Albert Whitman & Company,
visit our web site at www.albertwhitman.com

Little Rex, Big Brother

Big Brother

Ruth Symes

Illustrated by Sean Julian

Albert Whitman & Company • Chicago, Illinois

Rex was the
SCARIEST
dinosaur in the
whole world.

He had the pointiest of
pointy teeth,
the sharpest of sharp claws,

and the LOUDEST
of LOUD ROARS.

"Better watch out when Rex is about!" Rex growled fiercely to his reflection in the lake one day.

"You'll have to do better than that if you want to scare us!" said his friends Spikey and Three-Horns.

"Dear little Rex, we love you," said Rex's mom and dad, who were looking after the eggs nearby.

"I'm not little, **I'm BIG!**" shouted Rex. "Just you wait. I'll show you!"

Rex's Auntie Fang and Uncle Claw were
wading in the lake when suddenly—
"I'm a mud monster and I'll eat you!"
growled the meanest mud monster in the whole world.

"Be careful you don't get mud in your eyes, Rex,"
said Auntie Fang.
"You're such a funny little tyrannosaurus,"
said Uncle Claw.
"I'm not little," snapped Rex.
"I'm BIG and scary!"

That afternoon Spikey and
Three-Horns were having
a jumping contest.
Rex ran as fast as he could
and he jumped as high as he could.
He was the wildest jumping
dinosaur in the whole world.
But his pointy teeth got
caught on a tree branch.

"Owowowowowow!"

"You're too little to jump over
that high branch,"
said Spikey.

"I'm not little, I'm BIG!" shouted Rex.

But Spikey and Three-Horns couldn't understand him because his pointy teeth were still stuck in the branch.

Rex's mom and dad were looking after the eggs when there was a mighty roar from the bush beside them.

ROAR!

"Oh, there you are, Rex. Will you look after the eggs while we go for a swim?" asked Rex's mom.

Rex liked looking after the eggs.
It was a very important job.
"OK," he said. "But did I scare you? Say I scared you."
"We were *terrified*," said Rex's dad, smiling.

"Dear little Rex, we love you," said Rex's mom.
"We'll be back soon."

"I'm not little, I'm BIG!" called Rex.

Rex lay down next to the eggs. It was a hot
day, and he soon started to feel very sleepy.
TIP TIP TAP TAP.
Rex opened one eye and looked
left, and then he opened the
other eye and looked right.
What could that noise be?

TIP TIP TAP TAP.
Rex looked up,

and Rex looked down.
TIP TIP TAP TAP.
TAP TAP TIP TIP.

TIPPETY TAPPETY, TAPPETY TIPPETY.
More tips
and more taps.
More taps
and more tips.

And suddenly Rex
knew just what all those
tips and taps must be . . .

Baby dinosaurs hatching!

TIP TAP POP, went the first egg.

TAP TIP CRACK, went the second egg.

TIP TAP PING, went the third.

Rex was so excited.

"Hello, hello, hello!" he said.

But as soon as the baby dinosaurs saw Rex,
they tried to jump back into their shells.

"HELP!"

"He's so big!"

"I'm so scared!"

"No, no! Don't be scared.
I'm not big, I'm little," Rex said.
Rex didn't want to be the biggest,
scariest, loudest dinosaur anymore.
All Rex wanted to be was
the best dinosaur big brother
in the whole world.

And he was!